FIGHT FOR DUSTY DIVOT

AN UNOFFICIAL NOVEL OF FORTNITE

Trapped in Battle Royale
Book Five

FIGHT FOR DUSTY DIVOT

AN UNOFFICIAL NOVEL OF FORTNITE

Devin Hunter

Sky Pony Press
New York

Copyright © 2019 by Hollan Publishing, Inc.

Fortnite® is a registered trademark of Epic Games, Inc.
The Fortnite game is copyright © Epic Games, Inc.

Sky Pony Press books may be purchased in bulk at special discounts for sales promotion, corporate gifts, fund-raising, or educational purposes. Special editions can also be created to specifications. For details, contact the Special Sales Department, Sky Pony Press, 307 West 36th Street, 11th Floor, New York, NY 10018 or info@skyhorsepublishing.com.

Sky Pony® is a registered trademark of Skyhorse Publishing, Inc.®, a Delaware corporation.

Visit our website at www.skyponypress.com.

10 9 8 7 6 5 4 3 2

Library of Congress Cataloging-in-Publication Data is available on file.

Cover art by Amanda Brack
Series design by Brian Peterson

Paperback ISBN: 978-1-5107-4348-9
E-book ISBN: 978-1-5107-4349-6

Printed in the United States of America

CHAPTER 1

Retail Row was always an unpredictable place to land, but Grey and his squad had gotten lucky this battle. Even though ten players total landed there, Grey's squad had already taken out four of them. There were two more, but they were slippery.

"One by taco shop," Kiri said. "They're moving to the houses."

"Chase them," Grey said. Even if it was a top duo team, he was confident they could take the fight this early on. Grey's squad would have more gear, and no one had a lot of materials to initiate a build fight.

Taking out a higher-ranking duo early in the battle would only help Grey's rank.

Grey was tempted to use a bounce pad to get to them faster, but he needed to save them for later. Even having practiced with Lam's top-ten squad, it was still a challenge to fight against Lam and her late-game building strategies. A full inventory of all the tricks was the bare minimum needed to have a chance against them.

The house area of Retail Row was quiet by the time they got there. Everyone had landed in the stores, so the place appeared untouched. Grey scanned the houses, trying to see any movement or evidence of the players.

"You think they left?" Hazel asked. "They could have bailed."

"Maybe," Grey said. "If they're lower ranked they probably did, but if they're higher, they'll probably hide and get a flank on us when the storm comes in."

"Should we split up?" Finn asked.

"Yeah," Grey said as he moved past the first gray brick house by the taco place. "Finn, Hazel, you scout behind to see if they ran. Me and Kiri will watch the housefronts for a second."

"On it." Hazel headed west to where the next circle would be, and Finn followed her.

Grey and Kiri spread out a little as they looked

through windows in hopes of seeing someone. Using walls to give him protection from a possible sniper, Grey also listened to see if he could hear enemy footsteps in the houses. If the players were crouching, they would be too quiet to hear, but they could be rushing to gather more loot. Grey would hear them then.

The quiet moments drove Grey crazy with anticipation. They were almost worse than the chaos of fights. He hated those moments when he didn't know where the next attack might come from.

"Don't see anyone out here," Finn reported.

"In the red brick house!" Kiri said. "I hear footsteps from—no!"

The suction sound of a clinger grenade registered in Grey's ears, and just as he turned, he saw it explode on Kiri. She was knocked down immediately, and Grey rushed over in hopes to protect her from being eliminated.

He spotted the player on the roof and opened fire with an AR. The shots hit, and the guy backed off for a moment. "Get behind the fence!"

"Going as fast as I can," Kiri replied as her avatar crawled behind the meager defense.

Grey built a box around them, but the

players on the house opened fire. He replaced the walls they broke, but he had no time to revive Kiri. Her knocked-down health slowly dwindled. If he didn't get her revived soon, she'd be eliminated.

"Keep boxing in," Hazel said. "We're coming at them from behind."

The sound of more shots being fired told Grey that Finn and Hazel were there. He couldn't tell how the fight was going, but his walls weren't being destroyed, so he started reviving Kiri.

"Thanks, mate," Kiri said as her avatar stood back up.

"No prob." Grey dropped his bandages for her to use, and she also used a couple of small shield potions.

Finn eliminated Yuri.

Finn eliminated Vlad.

"Always taking my elims," Hazel grumbled.

"We're a team!" Finn replied. "It doesn't matter who gets them as long as we're all alive."

"Yeah it does—they determine our rank in squad," Hazel replied. "Even if we win, we all get our own rank in this version."

"There's not much difference between rank one and four. They're all good," Finn said.

"There is when you want to get home," Hazel replied.

"Focus, guys," Grey said. While Finn and Hazel mostly got along, sometimes competitiveness would get the better of them. "We're coming up there to work out the loot before we move."

After finding Finn and Hazel on the roof, Grey picked up the purple AR and left the green one he'd first gotten. He glanced at the icons at the top right of his vision to see how many people were still left on the map. It was already down to sixty.

"Not a bad start," Finn said as he grabbed the med kit to heal himself. Vlad and Yuri had nearly knocked him down in that fight. "Anyone got a big shield?"

"Me." Hazel dropped the large shield potion for Finn, grabbing the small potions instead. She took the purple rocket launcher from the pile of loot. "All your rocket ammo is mine."

"Sure, mate. I picked up some." Kiri handed over the rockets she had, and then it was time to move. The second storm was already moving in, and they were outside the safe zone.

Grey took a deep breath. "On to Dusty Divot. Stay focused."

Grey didn't like going to Dusty Divot. It wasn't nearly as treacherous as Tilted Towers, but it held its own dangers. The terrain was wide open, since the area was a giant crater in the ground. At the bottom of the crater was what looked like some sort of lab for experiments. While the loot was pretty good, Grey always felt like a fish in a barrel when they were down there.

Inevitably, someone would snipe you from the top of the crater.

With the loot they already had, Grey intended to be the squad sniping from the high vantage point rather than going down to loot the lab.

Gunfire could be heard in the distance, but it wasn't near their location. Grey figured someone was fighting near the border of the safe zone, and he prepared himself for a fight. But as Grey's squad ran west over the bright green terrain, a loud, unfamiliar sound overtook the pounding of their footsteps and the gunfire.

"What the heck is that?" Finn yelled as he stopped in his tracks.

Grey panicked as he looked for an enemy, but then he saw what Finn was referring to. There was a plume of smoke in the distance that continued to rise into the sky.

"The rocket!" Kiri said. "The Admin said it would launch soon!"

"I don't see what the big deal—" Hazel began. But before she could finish speaking, the rocket exploded and started falling back toward the ground.

Grey couldn't help but watch in fascination, even though part of him worried that they would be attacked while they stood there. He hoped everyone else was equally riveted and watching the rocket.

"What . . . ?" Finn said as a red laser appeared from the rocket.

"This is weird," Hazel said. "I don't think anything like this has happened in the game before."

A crashing bass sound pounded through the area as a flash of light cracked in the distance. Grey thought it was over Tilted Towers, but he couldn't tell from their current position. The rocket was gone, but then another flash and it appeared somewhere else on the map, and then somewhere else. Before he could begin to figure out what it meant, the rocket soared back into the air, and a massive explosion shattered the sky.

"Whoaaaaa!" Finn yelled as they all stared at the giant cracks left in the atmosphere.

Grey's mouth hung open as the cracks shone like broken glass. The island was silent after the whirring bass sound. Everyone had stopped fighting. They were all watching this in shock.

"What do you think it means?" Kiri asked.

"It means changes," Hazel said. "I don't know what kind, but it looks bigger than anything I've seen before."

"This is so cool!" Finn's avatar was jumping up and down in excitement, since Grey had banned him from dancing until after a victory. "I bet that crack is gonna do some cool stuff. The map will change for sure. I can't wait to see what the developers do."

Grey was silent. The rocket launch wasn't exciting for him, but scary. It signaled that the season was soon coming to an end. It said he was running out of time to get to the top five. It only reminded him that he might not get home this season.

CHAPTER 2

Grey's squad finished in the top fifteen for the battle. When they were teleported back to the warehouse with all the other players, everyone was in a commotion about the rocket. It was only the third battle of the day, so people gathered together to discuss their theories of what the rocket's explosion locations might mean.

"I hope they get rid of Loot Lake," Finn said. "I hate that place."

"The name is completely misleading," Hazel said. "But I'm for losing Haunted Hills. It's just so random."

"It'd be nice if it was Tilted Towers," Kiri said. "It's too popular."

"No!" Finn replied. "Tilted is the best!"

Grey sighed. He didn't want to talk about the rocket or what might change. He didn't want to think about the next season of this game. "None of that matters—the fights matter. Let's go practice."

Finn frowned. "Maybe it doesn't matter in fights, but it's still fun to think about. This is a game. You're supposed to have fun playing it."

Grey didn't reply. Though Finn had some complaints about the game, he was still way happier to be stuck in it than Grey was. Grey tried not to ruin his best friend's fun, but he also needed Finn to stay on task.

Kiri spoke instead. "I'd have much more fun if I wasn't stuck here and forced to play, but sure, I can see the fun in the changes."

"I'd rather see them on the computer screen," Hazel admitted.

Finn shook his head. "You guys are weird. *We're in a video game!* It's better than any theme park!"

Kiri gave Finn a tight smile before turning to Grey. "What do you want to practice?"

"Editing," Grey said. "We need to be ready for practice with Lam's squad tonight."

Finn groaned. "Editing is so boring."

"But replacing enemy walls and knowing how to edit yours will save you," Grey replied. "All of Lam's squad are great at it. I can't do it all for us. I might not always be right next to you."

"I know," Finn said. "I just wish we could practice close-range fights or something exciting instead."

"We will—that's important in build fights, too," Grey said in hopes of pacifying Finn. "During the next break, okay?"

Finn nodded. "Deal."

Grey and his squad went to the practice area, which was nearly deserted save the top twenty players. Everyone else had given up for the season, since most people didn't have a chance to up their average ranking with less than two weeks left in the season. It was only the top twenty who still had the chance to make or stay in the top five.

Tension was in the air as Grey eyed Zach's full squad, Vlad and Yuri's duo, and Lam's trio. Things had calmed down since the Admin banned bounties after Grey had reported Zach. The bounty Zach issued had caused players to hunt down Grey's squad using the spectator mode after being eliminated. One player would eliminate themselves and then report to their squad on where Grey's team was. Grey and his team had no chance to win with so many hunting them down. It was cheating, and Grey was proud he'd had the courage to report and put a stop to it. But that didn't mean the competition wasn't still fierce. In fact, the top twenty were practicing harder than ever now that it was a fair fight.

Hans's squad wasn't in sight, but Grey was sure they were off somewhere practicing. Tae Min never practiced. And the other two in the top twenty, Mason and Josh, a duo who just made it to ranks twenty and nineteen, were also missing.

When Lam spotted Grey, she walked over to him. "Still on for practice later?"

Grey nodded. "We are if you are."

"Good. I have some ideas I need to test." Lam might have offered to practice with Grey, but it wasn't the same sort-of-friendly fighting as it had been with other squads. Lam didn't play the social games the others did. Grey knew exactly why Lam asked for practice—to make sure she could continue to beat him. And he'd accepted in hopes of figuring out how to beat her.

The practices were rigorous, but Grey loved

how challenging they were. He was forced to think harder, to push himself, and that made his whole squad better.

Lam leaned in to whisper, "Meet at the forest past the ghost town this time."

"Got it." Grey and Lam had changed up their practice locations, since spying had become a thing. Bounties were gone, but someone had been bribing lower-ranked players to watch practices and report back.

After Grey's squad loaded up on loot from the practice warehouse, they headed out to the nearest open field. Grey wasn't as worried about spies for this, since it was more of a timed test than a strategy practice. "Okay, we'll take turns calling out types of edits, and everyone put them in your walls as fast as you can. First to edit will get a point. You get ten and you get to call the edits."

"We all know you'll win," Finn said.

"And I'll lose almost every round," Kiri said.

"It's not about winning. It's about getting faster at this so we can all be at our best," Grey said. "I'll call first. Build your walls."

Kiri, Finn, and Hazel placed their walls, waiting with their blueprints out to hear which edit

Grey would call. Grey waited a few minutes to build their anticipation. "Mid window."

They each edited to make a window in the middle of their wall.

"Hazel was first," Grey announced. "Door."

The windows disappeared and were replaced by doors. Finn got it first on this round. Grey continued to call out different types of edits for walls—bottom triangles, top arches, windows, doors. Then they moved on to ramp and floor edits. Though it wasn't exciting training, Grey had seen their improvement. Editing needed to become second nature for all of them.

"That's good for now," Grey said as the next battle approached.

They began walking back to the practice warehouse, but before they got there, Grey saw a commotion in front of the building.

It was Zach's squad.

It looked like they were arguing. Several groups had gathered to watch. Grey and his squad walked faster to hear what was going on.

" . . . can't do this to us, man!" Tristan yelled.

"Why are you blaming this on us?" Ben asked. "We gave you all our tips—it's your fault for not coming up with more strategies!"

"Yeah, you relied on the bounty instead!" Tristan said.

"Your tips weren't even yours, were they? You ran out because Grey taught you everything," Zach snapped back.

Ben and Tristan didn't have a reply for that.

"You can blame me if you want," Zach said as he folded his arms. "But it won't change the fact that me and Hui Yin can do better without you. You're just pulling down our ranks at this point 'cause we always have to babysit you."

"I'm tired of reviving you," Hui Yin added. "We've lost ranks trying to keep you two alive."

"We revive you all the time!" Ben said. Grey felt bad for Ben, who was the first person to befriend him in the game. He could tell his old friend was trying to hold back his emotions, but it wasn't working. Was their squad really breaking up when the end of the season was so close? Zach's squad hovered between top ten and just below, much like Grey's squad. If they broke up, chances were Grey could get his squad into the top ten.

But Ben and Tristan would be ruined.

They had worked so hard and given up so much to get a chance at the top five. Grey felt genuinely bad for them, but there wasn't a lot he could do. There were no six-person squads in this game.

"We're done," Zach said. "Go find someone else to leech off of."

Zach and Hui Yin walked away from Grey's old squad mates. Ben and Tristan tried to hold it together, but it was obvious they were devastated. Tristan balled his fists so tightly that it looked like he might punch something. Ben was already walking off, hiding his face from all the onlookers.

"I feel bad . . ." Kiri said quietly.

"Serves them right," Hazel said. "They played dirty, and it's coming back for them."

Kiri shot a glare at Hazel. "And you didn't?"

"What did I do?" Hazel shook her head. "Yeah, I insulted you, but I haven't lied to you or betrayed you or put bounties on you. If I did leave, I'd tell you straight up. If I didn't like how stuff was going in this squad, you'd hear it. It just so happens that Grey is way smarter than I predicted."

"Thanks . . . I think," Grey replied. "But in the end, it's not our business anymore. We gotta focus on our own stuff."

"Exactly," Finn said. "All this drama is annoying."

It was annoying, and Grey tried to avoid it at all costs. But he had grown a lot in the last six weeks and knew that Zach's squad breaking up would probably cause a chain reaction of squad shifts. He prepared for the reality that something could happen to his own squad—he wouldn't make that mistake twice.

CHAPTER 3

Since Zach's squad had split and didn't pose a threat, the last two games of the day went better than usual. Zach and Hui Yin still put up a decent fight as two, but they were never able to get more than one of Grey's squad members knocked down. Grey's squad took one victory, and Lam's squad took the other. As everyone teleported back to the battle warehouse for the end of the day, Grey could barely believe what he saw on the rankings board.

Tae Min wasn't ranked first.

It was Lam instead.

"Yes!" Lam jumped up and down as she stood in her first place position. "Finally!"

Tae Min was now right behind with a smile on his face. "Enjoy it while you can."

That peeled the grin right off Lam's face. "I'm keeping it."

"Maybe," was all Tae Min said.

Grey was sitting in tenth for the day, with Zach and Hui Yin right ahead. Ben and Tristan were right behind him. It was awkward to say the least, since he could feel his former squad mates glaring past him at Zach.

"You stalked us down on purpose, didn't you?" Tristan said.

"Of course I did," Zach replied. "Blame Grey. He made this a fair game, and you two don't have the skill to get home."

"Don't blame me," Grey said. "It's not my fault you can't bring out the best in your squad."

"Oh, is that how it's gonna be?" Zach asked.

Grey wished he had bitten his tongue, but he knew Ben and Tristan had the skills. They just needed the right coaching. "Leaders shouldn't blame their squad—they should question themselves first."

"You think you're so great now . . ." Zach grumbled. "You're just a kid who's gotten lucky."

"He's a kid who works hard and is good at the game," Hazel said. "You wouldn't have put a bounty on us if you thought it was luck."

Zach didn't have a reply to that.

The Admin appeared to finish off the day. She smiled wide. "Day Fifty of Battles has come to an end! As you all saw, the rocket has been launched and left cracks in the atmosphere. Be on the lookout for further hints of what is to come. We hope you will enjoy the changes we have prepared for you next season. There have been no reports. You are now free to use the practice area as usual."

Once the Admin left, everyone split off into their squads. While Grey and the other top twenty went off for yet another practice, everyone else looked like they were meeting up to have fun as friends. People who had once been tough and competitive, like Hazel's old squad and even Lorenzo's, had given up and were now hanging out around the cabins.

Grey pressed forward. They had practice with Lam's squad.

Though not many people went to the practice area, everyone who did eyed each other. People didn't practice out front anymore. Everyone would be able to see. No one practiced together except for Lam's and Grey's squads. Grey figured it wouldn't last for long. Maybe a few more days and Lam would say that was enough.

Grey would take it while he could. He'd already learned a lot from Lam, even if she had also taken some of his ideas.

After Grey and his squad gathered their items and materials, they hiked out to the remote spot Lam had chosen for practice. This forest was past the ghost town, and they walked so deep into it that they were near the barrier of the game much like in the other forest Grey liked to go to. He had discovered that the whole area was surrounded by forest and barriers. It reminded him of the storm in the battles, except that it never moved and you couldn't pass through it.

"What's the plan today?" Grey asked as they approached Lam's squad. She was all business, so Grey tried to match that with as little small talk as possible.

"Fun house," Lam answered. "You make one first."

"Sure thing." Grey had done this practice with Lam's squad before—it was something she had come up with but he liked to do. One team would have a couple minutes to build a maze of boxes and ramps and towers, outfit it with whatever traps and bouncers they wanted, and then the other team would have to infiltrate it and try to eliminate the players inside.

Whether Grey's squad was the one building or hunting, it was always a challenge and a good lesson.

Once Lam's squad had moved far enough away not to see what Grey's squad was doing, Grey said, "Let's all build our own and see what they do. They'll have to guess who is where and maybe it'll give us an advantage."

"What if we all build one, and then we pick one to hide in together?" Kiri suggested.

Grey smiled. "I like that. We could get the jump on them if they pick the wrong one."

"What kind of build? Identical?" Hazel asked.

Grey pursed his lips. "It's a good idea, but we don't have time to decide on the build right now. Maybe next round. Do what you want this time. Build and then meet in Finn's structure."

"Got it." Hazel ran to a different spot and began to build.

"We should hide in your building," Finn said

as he began to throw down walls in front of him, Grey, and Kiri. "It'll be the best one."

"But that's the one they'll pick if Lam thinks it looks like my build," Grey said.

"Good point," Finn said. "Better hurry."

"Right." Grey ran away from Finn's build while Kiri went past where Hazel was building.

Grey started by building the base of a one-by-one tower, but then he added ramps and boxes all around it. In some of the boxes he placed traps, and as he built higher, he added some bounce pads as well. These might not cause damage if someone fell, but they would cause chaos and also potentially give his allies a way to escape a fight as well.

He tried not to think about the logic of his build, since he knew they'd be moving to Finn's anyway. He had noticed that Lam thrived on logical builds, and sometimes it was better for it to appear as if someone with less skill had made the fun house.

A loud sniper shot echoed through the forest, indicating that the time to build had run out. Lam's squad would be on the way.

Grey dropped one bounce pad at the top of his fun house and used it to get over to Finn's tower faster. Since they were in practice mode, he could see his squad's names over their heads and knew everyone else was already in the tower. But the downside of practice mode was that they didn't have the private communication system they had in the battles. If they spoke, Lam's squad would potentially hear them.

This practice was all about being quiet.

Once Grey landed in Finn's tower, he crouched to reduce his footstep noise as much as possible. He hid behind a ramp, pleased to see that Finn had placed a trap behind it.

Grey couldn't immediately hear Lam's squad approach, and he wondered if they had paused in confusion when they saw the multiple buildings they would have to choose from. He hoped so. Impressing Lam was nearly as good as impressing Tae Min.

Once Lam's squad got close enough, he could hear their footsteps change from the sound of walking on grass to walking on wood. So they had picked a fun house to explore.

Grey peeked between the wood slats, trying to figure out which building Lam's squad was in. As he did, he began to worry this wasn't the best strategy. Maybe Lam wouldn't immediately find them, but Lam might be able to use the towers Grey's squad built to her advantage.

If this strategy was to work, Grey's squad would have to be aggressive. Except he couldn't tell them when to attack without the coms—he would have to hope he had taught them enough that they would know.

Or at least follow his lead.

Grey caught movement in his own tower. He planned to use the clinger grenades he had picked up to launch his attack, but then he heard a rocket launch from nearby. He saw it soar into Hazel's tower, not his.

Lam's squad must have split up.

And if they did . . .

Grey launched all his clingers at the tower he'd built, hoping that would direct his squad to pay attention to both buildings. Then he began to move down Finn's tower because he was sure someone from Lam's squad would be on their way here the moment they saw the rocket.

They would definitely try to bring the whole thing down. Lam's squad was never ashamed to take advantage of the powerful explosives in the game. Especially now that so many other weapons had been nerfed. Grey had to get down to the lower levels and eliminate that person before his whole team was down because of fall damage.

Grenades and rockets flew through the air as Grey used his materials to drop down to the ground. The other structures he and his squad had built were in shambles, but he wasn't sure Lam's squad members had gone down in the flurry. Chances were, they had backed out enough to build their own defensive measures.

Grey ran around Finn's tower trying to find evidence of the enemies. While he didn't see anyone, he did see something worse—a C4 planted on a wall.

He heard the click of another C4 being placed, and he panicked. Maybe he could build more walls to keep the tower standing . . . but Lam's squad would just have more C4 to take those walls down, too.

That was when Grey remembered C4 could damage the person who placed it as well. He realized there was another option: explode the C4 by shooting it.

He quietly moved to the edge of a wall and peeked behind. It was a risk since the C4 could explode at any second, but he had to do it. He spotted Lam throwing another explosive and took the shot, hoping he'd hit the C4 in the air and it would explode in Lam's face.

He missed.

Lam startled at the shot but then triggered the C4. The whole building went down, and Grey took a hit that he knew would have eliminated him. Grey's squad all dropped to the ground around him.

"You and your C4!" Finn said to Lam.

Lam only smiled at Grey. "You nearly had me. Building multiple towers was clever, though."

"Yeah . . ." Grey sat on the ground, disappointed even though it was only practice. If that had been a real game, it would have been one more they would have lost. One more that would have put Lam's squad in the lead. Grey and his friends couldn't afford to lose anymore. Every loss could ruin their chance of getting home. "Guess I need to work on my aim."

"Nah," Lam said. "It's already bad enough that you figured out I'd be down here."

"We'll get you next time," Kiri said.

"Maybe. We'll clear the towers over there." Lam headed over to where Pilar and Trevor were already breaking down the rest of Hazel's building.

Grey's squad broke down his tower and then moved out to await their turn for hunting. He tried to shake off the loss, but it was getting harder and harder to do. "We need to win this next one, guys."

"We'll do our best," Kiri said.

He stopped. "I need more than that—if we can't beat them in practice, we'll never beat them in battles. And that means we're not going home."

Kiri gave him a look he couldn't place. "I know, mate. No need to get angry."

"Sorry. Just pretend like it's a real game from now on," Grey said.

"I always do," Finn said.

"Me too," Hazel said. "You're not the only one who wants to go home, Grey. Don't act like we're slackers just because Lam can beat you."

The words hit a chord in Grey, and not a good one. He realized he was on the verge of tilting, and he needed to be careful that the pressure didn't make him crack. Because if he couldn't hold it together, chances were his whole squad would fall apart.

CHAPTER 4

The next day came faster than Grey wanted it to. He couldn't stop thinking about yesterday's practices with Lam and how often they lost. Had it been a mistake to practice with Lam's squad? It felt like she had figured out Grey's strategies much faster than he'd learned any of hers. Maybe they should stop practicing with her. Grey wasn't sure what the right decision was.

"You seem troubled," Tae Min said.

Grey startled, not having realized that people were moving around him as he sat thinking. The cabin had been emptied except for him and Tae Min. "Oh, yeah . . . I guess I am. But isn't everyone who is trying to make the top five feeling troubled?"

"Probably." Tae Min came over and sat by Grey on his bed. "But you are thinking of something specific."

There was no point in hiding stuff from Tae Min, who was usually willing to help in his cryptic way. "I'm trying to decide if I should stop practicing with Lam's squad. We keep losing. She's figuring me out instead of the other way around."

"You think so?" Tae Min asked. "Or are you playing her game instead of yours?"

Grey raised an eyebrow. "What do you mean?"

Tae Min shrugged. "Perhaps you have her more figured out than you think, but you're trying to fight her with her own tactics. It seems that you believe she is smarter than you."

"She is." Grey was certain of it. He was certain anyone else would agree. "She's a lot older than me. And her strategies are winning her this game. I don't win against her squad enough to surpass them."

"Almost everyone here is older than you," Tae Min pointed out. "What makes her so special?"

Grey didn't want to say it out loud. He thought Lam was smart. He thought she was a good player. He admired the way she played the game and had learned a lot from her.

"Don't try to be Lam," Tae Min finally said when Grey let the silence go on too long. "You're not Lam. You're Grey. If you keep trying to beat her with her own strategies, of course she will win. She knows her play style more than anyone else could. Even if you've learned to mimic it, she will always have a leg up."

"I'm not trying to be her," Grey said.

"You are." Tae Min got up and headed for the door. "Think about it. You haven't been trying to get better at what you do best—you've been trying to be someone you're not. How would Grey beat Lam? You've beaten her before, and I have a feeling those times weren't when you were trying to be her."

Tae Min left Grey alone after that. Grey stayed there to think. Was he really trying to be like Lam? He hadn't thought of it that way, but if Tae Min said he was, then Grey had to consider the possibility.

When Grey's squad had practiced with other squads, had he done the same thing? Had he tried to be like Hans or Zach or Lorenzo? Now that he thought about it . . . he didn't. Grey had tried to *counter* them. But with Lam, Grey was trying to build like she would build. He was trying to place traps and explosives and bouncers where she might place them. Because he thought she did it better than he did.

Embarrassment washed over him. Tae Min had seen Grey's admiration easily, and he worried that everyone else saw it too. In fact, he was almost certain that Lam saw it most of all. She had used his fascination with her strategies to distract him from his own strengths. He'd almost forgotten what he was good at in just a few days.

Tae Min was right, as usual. Grey needed to play his way. He needed to find a way to counter Lam's strategies that worked for him. And it wouldn't be copying her style.

Just as Grey was about to go find his squad, someone else entered the cabin. Grey's eyes grew wide at the figure. "Lam."

"Hey," she said as she looked around the room. "Sounds like you and Tae Min are pretty friendly. I would have never guessed."

"You were listening?" Grey gulped, suddenly even more nervous than before. Would Lam tell others about Tae Min? Why did Grey feel like he'd be in trouble if other people knew?

"Of course I was." Lam sat on Lorenzo's bed, which was right across from Grey's. "It wasn't on purpose, though. I was on my way here to ask you to join my squad."

Grey stared at her. He couldn't have heard right. "What?"

"You'd be guaranteed a spot home," Lam said. "No one could challenge our squad if you were on it, too."

She was right, and Grey knew it. If he joined with Lam, he'd sail right on home. His squad wouldn't be able to beat them. All the others were already broken and weak.

But he would have to abandon his squad. His friends.

Grey had been asked a couple times to join squads, but it had been easy to say no. This time it felt harder. They were so close to the end of the season. There wasn't time to improve, and Grey needed to win more battles than lose.

Part of him wanted to say yes. It was like Ben and Tristan had said—what's most important is getting *yourself* home.

But the bigger part of him knew he'd always regret leaving his friends behind, even if he never got such an easy chance again. So he said, "I can't. Sorry. You can probably get Ben or Tristan. Both of them really want to go home."

Lam glared at him. "I'm not handing out charity. They're already out of my way. I need your squad out of my way. The only reason we're practicing is so I could see which person was the best to steal. That's you. But if you don't join me, I'll just get one of your squad members instead."

Grey knew their practices weren't friendly, but he still didn't expect Lam to try and steal his squad members. "So much for fair competition, huh?"

"It's fair to get the best team possible," Lam said. "And *you* can take Ben or Tristan back on if you want. Or do you think they're worse than your current team?"

"They aren't." Grey balled his fists, so angry he hadn't seen it sooner. He'd been so blinded by his desire to learn Lam's style that he hadn't realized she was out to sabotage him like this. It might be too late to recover if she succeeded. "I'll beat you no matter who is in my squad."

Lam laughed at that. "No, you won't. I'm gonna go find Kiri."

"Leave my squad alone!" Fear set in as he realized Lam's offer could be just as tempting to the

rest of his squad. And if he lost any of them now
. . . "Why won't any of you play fair?"

"Because fair hasn't gotten us anywhere,"
Lam said. "Haven't you figured that out yet?"

"Yeah, but I want to prove you all wrong,"
Grey said. "It can be fair."

"Why can't you join my squad and be done
with it?" Lam asked, and just as she did, someone
else came through the door.

Kiri.

She didn't look happy. Grey's eyes went wide
as he realized she'd probably heard Lam's offer.

CHAPTER 5

Lam smiled when she saw Kiri had come in. "Kiri, just who I wanted to talk to."

Kiri didn't look at her but instead stared down Grey. "So are you leaving us? Is that what I walked in on?"

"He said no." Lam put her hand on Kiri's shoulder to get her attention. "But if you want to take my offer, I'd be more than happy to have a sniper of your caliber."

"That was your plan all along, ay?" Kiri pointed to the door. "Get out."

Lam shrugged as she went to leave. "Offer stands. I'll go find Finn and Hazel."

"Don't you dare!" Kiri yelled after her. She

turned back to Grey. "Please tell me this is the first time she's done this."

He nodded. "I said no. Why are you mad at me?"

"I'm not. I'm mad that she did this. I want to believe people will play fair and . . ." Kiri put her hands on her hips. "I'm glad you said no. It wasn't easy, was it?"

Grey shook his head. "Is it easy for you to say no?"

"It's hard," Kiri admitted. "Especially now."

"You think Finn or Hazel will take her up on it?" Grey asked.

Kiri pursed her lips as she thought. "I don't think Finn will—he hates that sort of play style, and he's your mate in real life. But Hazel . . . I dunno. She's scared to stay here another season."

Grey let out a sigh. He remembered when Hazel told him she didn't have anyone in the real world, how she was afraid she might die if she was in a coma too long. If any of them might take Lam's offer, it would be Hazel. "So much for not having any drama in our squad."

"If we don't make drama, it comes to us anyway," Kiri grumbled.

"Let's find them quick." Grey rushed out of his cabin, hoping he could find Finn and Hazel before Lam did. He knew Lam wouldn't stop her quest to recruit someone from Grey's squad, but he hoped he could at least prevent it for a few more games. He needed his squad to focus on the game.

He needed them to stay in his squad.

Grey never thought he'd say it, but he didn't want Hazel to leave. She'd improved a lot, and she wasn't so mean anymore. He liked her and believed she made their squad better. Grey could find someone to replace Hazel, but he didn't want to. It would mean even more drama because he'd have to choose between Ben and Tristan. Leaving one of them out felt worse than leaving both out. They had been a team for so long.

Sure enough, Lam had found Finn by the campfire that was in the center of the cabin circle. Finn was laughing in Lam's face. Grey assumed Lam had already attempted to recruit him.

"Finn!" Grey called as he ran over.

"Hey, dude," Finn said as he pointed to Lam. "She thinks I'm gonna join her squad. Isn't that hilarious? Betray my best friend so I can hide out in boxes all game. Yeah, right!"

"Glad you feel that way." Grey looked around for Hazel's bright green hair, but he didn't see her anywhere. "Let's go talk strategy for today."

"Where's Hazel?" Lam asked.

"None of your business," Kiri said.

"We'll see you in the battles," Grey said. "Otherwise, stay away from us. Forget practicing."

Lam pretended to be sad. "Oh no, what will I do?" she said sarcastically.

Grey walked away from her. Finn and Kiri followed. Finn caught up to Grey and asked, "Did she ask you guys, too, or just me?"

"She asked me first and then Kiri," Grey answered as he went to find Hazel. He hoped she was already in the battle warehouse waiting for them. They usually went there at the start of each day to talk about their plan for the day.

"Ugh, not even first pick," Finn said. "Rude."

"She's messing with us," Grey replied. "Even if no one leaves, this is a distraction that will take our focus off beating her. We can't let mind games get to us."

"No problem here," Finn said. "Should we warn Hazel?"

Grey stopped before he got to the battle warehouse. He hadn't thought of warning Hazel that

Lam was trying to recruit. Even now, he was scared that if Hazel knew, she would decide to leave his squad right away. But if they kept it from her . . . she would probably think they didn't trust her.

Finally, Grey nodded. "Probably."

"You sure?" Kiri asked. "What if she leaves us right now?"

"Then we'll have to deal with it. I can't make anyone stay if they don't want to." Grey kept walking, and the moment he stepped inside, it wasn't hard to spot Hazel.

She sat at a table by herself, and when she saw them come in, she shouted, "What took you so long?"

Grey, Finn, and Kiri sat at the table, no one replying. Grey knew his friends thought he was the one who should tell her, but he struggled to say it.

Hazel's brow furrowed in the awkward silence. "Is something wrong? What happened?"

There was no reason to drag this out. Hazel would want Grey to tell it to her straight. "Lam is trying to recruit someone from our squad. She's asked us all, and now she's looking for you. She thinks recruiting one of us will tank our chances to beat her for the top spots."

"Oh . . ." Hazel's eyes brightened with more hope and interest than Grey wanted to see. "She'll take any of us?"

"Yeah," Grey said. "Learning our style, messing with us, and I guess this recruitment was all part of her plan to ensure she stays in the number-one rank. She thinks if we fall apart, there will be no one to challenge her squad."

Hazel leaned her elbows on the table, not looking at any of them. "She's right. They already beat us a ton with just three squad members. Taking one of us to her side would make them overpowering."

Grey struggled to talk past the lump in his throat. He could see what he feared—Hazel was seriously considering Lam's offer. "But this means she sees us as a threat to her position. I hope we can stay together and fight her for it. I think we can win. I promise I won't be hung up on her play style anymore. I got caught up in trying to be like her, and I shouldn't have done that. We should have kept doing our own thing, improving our own style, instead of me trying to copy hers."

Hazel pursed her lips as she thought. "I'm not gonna lie—Lam's offer is super tempting.

There's no way I can turn it down right here and now without thinking about it."

"I get that . . ." Grey said, though he was disappointed.

"I'm not saying I'll leave," Hazel said. "I'm just being honest that I can't ignore a guaranteed spot in the top five. No matter what I decide, I won't be like Ben and Tristan and just disappear, okay? That's the best I can promise right now."

Kiri let out a sigh. "I guess the honesty is nice, even if you clearly don't have faith in us."

"It's not about that," Hazel said. "Do I think we could do it? Yeah. I really do. But it's still a risk, you know? And a risk isn't a guarantee. It's hard to pass up on that. You can't tell me you weren't tempted, Kiri, when we're this close to the end."

Kiri frowned. "Of course it's tempting, but that doesn't make it right."

"Is it wrong, though?" Hazel asked.

Before any of them could answer, the daily announcement sounded throughout the area. *Battles begin in thirty seconds!*

"We can't worry about it now," Grey said before they were teleported to the line. "Let's do our best today to get Victory Royales—that will help us all no matter what people decide in the end, right?"

"Right," Hazel said. Finn and Kiri agreed, too.

But as the battles began, Grey didn't feel good at all. Even if everyone tried to do their best, the tone of the squad had already changed. Grey wasn't just on edge because of the competition— he was on edge because at any minute Hazel could decide to leave his squad and fight against them. A seed of distrust had been planted, and it would only grow from there.

CHAPTER 6

Despite Lam's attempt to make trouble in Grey's squad, they were able to win the first three games of the day. Zach and Hui Yin took the fourth. But Grey hoped those three Victory Royales would somehow convince Hazel to stick around as they faced the final battle of the day.

Instead of waiting until the end of the battles to fight Lam, Grey had tried to find her squad earlier. He knew how much Lam liked to load up on materials before she faced any fights, so he targeted places like Wailing Woods and Lonely Lodge where there were enough trees to fill an entire squad on wood materials.

He got lucky on three of the five games, having

found them early enough to take them out before they could build their fun houses. Tae Min was right—Grey needed to play his own game, and fighting out in the open favored Grey's squad.

But after the first three games, Lam stopped going to her farming spots and she was harder to track down.

"This loot sucks," Finn said as they finished picking over Wailing Woods.

"I know," Grey said as he broke down a nearby tree. "But it's worth it if we can get Lam's squad early."

"True," Kiri said. "Just those three early losses knocked her out of first."

"Not for long with Tae Min purposely tanking," Hazel pointed out. "He literally dove right into the sea this time to take the one hundredth rank."

"I miss him being godly," Finn said. "He was fun to fight."

"Yeah, it's not the same." Grey didn't know how an amazing player like Tae Min could accept those kinds of losses. Tae Min seemed like the kind of person who would hate to lose, even if he was doing it on purpose.

There were still fifty players left in this final

battle of the day, so Grey believed they had time to find Lam's squad before they got too geared up. He headed over to Tomato Town in search of better loot, and luckily there was some left, though it was obvious a fight had gone down. Piles of loot sat out in the open next to some small builds. The best gear had been taken by the winners of the fight, but there were still a few things that Grey's squad was happy to have, like a better sniper rifle for Kiri and a whole stack of small shields.

"Why'd they leave these behind?" Finn said as he grabbed the shields.

"Must have had big shields or a chug jug," Hazel said.

"We need to be careful if they do—whoever was here might be aggressive if they see us." Grey looked around. Tomato Town had been broken up, and there was evidence everywhere of looting, but he heard no one. He glanced at his mini-map. The storm was closing again soon. They needed to get west pronto.

"Lam will already be heading to the center of the safe zone," Kiri pointed out. "We'll be in for it."

Grey knew this was true, but there was nothing else to be done but face them. Hopefully he could find a way to defeat Lam's squad in his own way in the latter part of the battle. So far he'd only won when he caught them early. "Whatever we're in for, we'll need better loot than this."

"Seriously," Hazel said. "I still have all gray weapons."

"Let's try Anarchy Acres." It was a big farm in the northern part of the island. Much like Lucky Landing, it didn't get a lot of players because sometimes the storm circle would be hard to get to. In this battle, it was circling over Dusty Divot, so all they needed to do was rotate south after looting Anarchy Acres and eliminate anyone they might meet.

As they approached the east side of Anarchy Acres, Grey could tell that someone had been there gathering loot because the houses and barns had walls missing. But there wasn't much in the way of player-built structures, so there couldn't have been much fighting going on.

"Keep a lookout," Grey said. "They might still be here."

"We gotta be quick," Finn said. "Next storm starts in a minute."

"Let's split," Kiri said. "Me and Hazel, Grey and Finn."

"Good plan. We'll hit the west side." Grey moved cautiously across the open fields on his way to the other side of the farm. He scanned the area for any movement, but there was nothing.

When he and Finn entered the first building on their side, loot lay around open chests. Someone had been here and taken what they needed just like in Tomato Town, but there was a lot more left. There were clinger grenades, impulse grenades, and some med kits that would be useful.

"I hate getting leftovers," Finn grumbled as he upgraded his SMG from gray to blue. "And there aren't any traps or bouncers or launch pads for us."

"Yeah." Grey knew it was a big problem—those items always came in handy when fighting Lam's squad. "We need to find some people to eliminate. Maybe they'll have some."

"This has been a boring battle for sure." Finn peeked out a window to check for any other players, but by his groan, Grey knew he saw nothing. "Where is everyone? There are forty on the map still!"

"I don't know." Fortnite Battle Royale was strange like that. Sometimes Grey and his squad would land with plenty of enemies to fight right away, and sometimes it would be abandoned until they hit the smaller storm circles and were forced closer to their final opponents.

Just when Grey thought Finn might protest out of boredom, he heard the sound of SMG fire in the distance.

"There's a duo on us," Kiri said with a shockingly calm voice. "No sight of extra players."

"They're good. Might be Zach and Hui Yin," Hazel added.

"Or Ben and Tristan. Or Yuri and Vlad," Kiri said.

"Save some for me!" Finn ran out of the barn. Grey wanted to yell at him for being reckless, but he wasn't nearly as paranoid now that Tae Min wasn't around to snipe out of nowhere.

"Remember they have the better loot!" Grey called as he followed Finn toward the sound of the fight.

"It's all about how you use it," Finn claimed as he built himself a protective wall and ramp. They were playing cat and mouse outside and inside the farmhouse.

"The thief skin is low," Hazel said. "Got him good with my shotgun."

"I see him!" Finn opened fire, and it took no time to see the notification.

Finn knocked down Ben.

Kiri eliminated Tristan.

Once Kiri did that, Ben was also eliminated, and his loot spilled from his avatar like a piñata. Grey felt bad, but not too bad when he saw the good stuff they had. He wasn't surprised they'd pick a location on the outskirts—they would be trying to preserve their rank as much as possible, hoping they could still make top five when they were so close.

"Grab it all," Grey said. "Storm's coming."

They'd gained some of the tools they needed, so Grey considered it worth the risk even though they ended up getting caught in the storm and taking damage. They had enough healing to make it out, and the better loot allowed them to take out another lower-ranked squad on the way to Dusty Divot.

Lam eliminated Zach.

Pilar eliminated Hui Yin.

"Well, they must have found Lam's fortress," Finn said. "Two more out of the way."

"Yup." Though as they approached Dusty Divot, Grey watched the number of players dwindle. Many were taken out by Vlad and Yuri, but then they were ultimately taken down by Lam's squad as well. Whatever Lam had created for this battle, it had to be formidable. With all the losses Grey had handed her today, she had to have been out for revenge.

The crater was in sight, and Grey took shelter in the broken warehouses on the cliff. He peeked into the crater, expecting to see some elaborate fun house that Lam's squad had built in Dusty Divot, but to his surprise he saw nothing but the lab buildings. There was evidence of people having been there to fight, though it seemed more like small fights that ended quickly.

"Maybe they're not there . . ." Kiri offered.

"But this is where the safe zone will be," Finn said. "Lam always camps in the safe zone."

"We changed it up today," Hazel offered. "Maybe she did, too, after you beat her so much."

"Maybe . . ." Grey looked down at the lab again. He had a feeling they were being watched. "Kiri, stay here and protect yourself. Take shots if anyone shows."

"Aye, aye, Captain." Kiri began to build herself a small base, even if it was only Grey's squad and Lam's squad left.

"Down we go." Grey wasn't sure how to approach when there wasn't an obvious location to target. Lam usually made it obvious where they were, but maybe she had learned from yesterday's practice when Grey tried those decoy towers.

Grey expected to take some fire as they built their way down into the crater, but it was quiet. Too quiet. His squad's loud footsteps had to have told Lam's squad that he was there, and yet Lam's squad still didn't move. He didn't hear anything in the area to tell him where they were.

"Where are they?" Finn asked. "The storm is closing in again. They have to be here."

"They want us to play hide-and-seek," Hazel said.

"Yeah." Grey looked over the buildings, noticing that at any place there would have been a window, there was now a wall. It was a trap— one exactly like he'd built in their last practice— except Lam had used Dusty Divot's existing buildings to employ it. "How many explosives do we have?"

"Not enough," Hazel replied. "I have hand grenades. Finn has clingers."

If only they had C4 or a rocket launcher.

Grey would even take a grenade launcher at this point. But this would have to do. "Break some walls down. Maybe we'll find someone before we have to go in."

While Finn and Hazel used their explosives, Grey used his tommy gun to break down some walls in the nearest building. There was still no sign of Lam's squad.

"No!" Kiri yelled. "No, no, no! They're up here!"

Lam knocked down Kiri.

Lam eliminated Kiri.

Before Grey had time to react, he got hit with a sniper shot for almost all his health. He tried to take cover, but he was stuck in the crater. Lam had baited them down there, and Grey had fallen for it. He, Finn, and Hazel had been sitting ducks.

It wasn't hard for Lam to take the Victory Royale from there.

When they appeared back in the battle warehouse at the end of the day, Lam said, "And *that* is how you play the decoy game, Grey. Looks like I can beat you when you try a decoy *and* when I do it. I'm clearly the better leader, the one who can get players out of this game."

Grey pursed his lips. He wouldn't reply. Lam had gotten him, and it felt like all his efforts to prove himself that day meant nothing.

CHAPTER 7

After the Admin finished the day, there was no stopping Lam from taking Hazel aside to offer her a spot on the squad. Hazel seemed completely on the fence as she looked between Grey and Lam. He wanted to believe Hazel would stay, but more and more it felt like wishful thinking.

"She's not really going to switch squads, is she?" Kiri asked.

"I don't know, dude," Finn said. "My bet is she will."

"But we did so well today. Look at our ranks." Kiri pointed to the list on the battle warehouse's wall. They had all moved up into the top ten now, since Ben, Tristan, and Tae Min had moved down. There were only six people ahead of them. If they kept putting up that many victories in a day, they had a fighting chance.

If Hazel left . . . it'd all be gone.

"Hazel," Grey said. "Please stay with us. We're already close."

"Close isn't enough," Lam said. "One good day won't get you there. My squad has the higher average, and we will keep it that way. Hazel has a better chance to up her rank with us than with you."

"Your ranks won't last if she stays with us and you know it," Grey shot back. "That's why you're doing this to begin with!"

"Ugh!" Hazel yelled so loudly everyone could hear her. "Will you leave me alone for one second so I can think? You're both so obnoxious right now I'd rather join up with Zach and Hui Yin instead!"

"Sounds good to me!" Zach called from the table where he and Hui Yin sat, watching the drama unfold.

Hazel rolled her eyes and stomped off.

Grey sighed as he watched her go. How did drama always filter down from one squad to another? And at the worst times? He looked at

Finn and Kiri. "You want to practice your way, Finn? I don't want to sit around waiting for how this will go."

"Sure," Finn said with a wary smile. "You and Kiri are the ones who need the most practice in close combat anyway."

"You're not wrong," Kiri said as she began the too-familiar walk to the practice warehouse. "It's crazy to think I'd be gutted over Hazel leaving after she was so awful at first . . . but here we are. I'm not even complaining over close-combat practice, and I hate it."

"That's pretty serious," a surprising voice said from behind.

Grey turned to find Ben. He couldn't help but be shocked, and before he could think, he said, "What're you doing here? Gaming for a possible spot on my squad if Hazel leaves?"

Ben cringed. "No . . ."

"Then what?" Grey was being too harsh, but this game had changed him for better or worse. He hardly trusted anyone to say what they meant when so much was on the line.

Ben looked back at Tristan, who was leaning on a tree trunk a few yards back. Tristan was hard to read, but even so, he looked like he was too afraid to talk to Grey himself. "We know you won't take us back—and we're not looking to split up—but you three and us two makes five players. You think there's any way to form an alliance to get us all to the top five?"

Grey's brow furrowed as he thought about the proposition.

"Sorry, I shouldn't have asked . . ." Ben said as he backed up. "I know you don't like those kind of games. It's just that Tris—"

"No, that wasn't a glare," Grey interrupted. "I was thinking. It's an interesting idea. I'm just not sure how it would work."

Kiri stepped forward. "Can we think about it? It's not exactly easy to agree to something like that after you betrayed us, and it seems like every alliance has already fallen apart. I'm not sure any of us have enough trust left for something like that."

"That's completely fair," Ben said. "I know it's a lot more than I should ask after . . ."

"You left them high and dry?" Finn filled in. "Gotta be honest, I don't like you guys at all. Grey's my best friend, and all you did was use him because he's a nice person."

Ben nodded. "Yeah, well, I said what I came

to say. Hazel might stick with you anyway. But it's not like any of us have the time to sit on stuff. Gotta try and help our ranks if we have the chance."

It was true, though Grey wasn't sure if this was the way to do it. "We'll let you know after we find out what Hazel decides."

"Okay." Ben walked back to Tristan to relay the news.

"Can we do the fun practicing now?" Finn said.

"Yeah, dude, let's do this." Grey put his arm around Finn's shoulders, even more glad for a distraction now. "Teach us the ways of an aggressive player."

Finn laughed. "Will do."

After loading up on loot, they went down to the river to practice. It was strange for Grey not to be in charge, but it was nice, too. He didn't have to come up with the practices. All he had to do was listen to Finn and try to execute what his best friend requested.

"Nice hit!" Finn said as Grey flew through the air and landed on the ground several yards away. "See? You can do it when you're focused."

They had been practicing flying shots. Finn

had placed several bouncers at different heights, directing Grey and Kiri to hit him in his tower while flying. It was something they practiced occasionally, but Grey was never very good at it. Especially if his target was also moving.

"I feel like it's all luck," Grey said. "No one can actually hit these shots consistently."

Finn raised an eyebrow. "You're only saying that because you're bad at it. I can hit them a lot, and it's not luck. It's about timing, getting used to the fall speed, and knowing how to aim. You just don't like this kind of practice because you don't like risky plays."

Grey pursed his lips. "Yeah, I guess I don't see the point."

"The point is you can bounce in on people who like to hole up, and they usually aren't ready for it." Finn jumped down from his tower. "Think about it—our biggest enemies are turtles. We gotta get under their shells if we're gonna win."

"He has a point," Kiri said. "It does seem like Lam folds under aggression. Maybe it's not about breaking down the defense, but bypassing it altogether."

Grey folded his arms, thinking. "But sometimes I don't know how to bypass their defense."

"That's why we're doing this!" Finn said. "There are probably other ways too, but this works. Sometimes you gotta get that damage down before you even land. And you can also get behind them."

"Okay, okay," Grey said. "Let's keep doing this then. But can I try to counter you guys as you attempt to hit me? Because I think there are plenty of ways the enemy could protect from jump shots."

"Challenge accepted!" Finn replied.

"I'll give it my best," Kiri said.

Grey bounced into Finn's tower this time and prepared himself for the onslaught. He tried not to smile, but he already had the perfect plan for this.

Finn and Kiri began to jump on the various bouncers, and as they flew, they shot. Grey built walls to block the shots. Finn switched to a tommy gun, which burned down Grey's walls faster. He took a few hits, but it was nothing he wouldn't be able to withstand.

Grey knew Finn would get impatient if he couldn't hit Grey from a distance. So he waited for his friend to jump right at him.

Sure enough, it only took two more bounces for Finn to come flying at Grey. Grey built a ceiling onto his tower, and Finn shot at it to break it down. As he did, Grey placed a trap inside and then edited the ceiling so that Finn would fall through.

The trap spikes sprung out the moment Finn's feet hit the floor. He would have taken nearly fatal damage from that alone, and Grey held up his shotgun. "Gotcha."

Finn shook his head. "Well played. But let's do it again. I have a plan."

The next time, Finn didn't land right on top of Grey but instead built a floor on top of Grey as he flew. He landed on Grey's box, but this time Finn was in control of the floor he made. While Grey tried to shoot it down, Finn edited a corner open and got Grey.

"Smart change," Grey replied.

Kiri landed on the tower, too. "You could drop a trap in there even."

"True," Finn said.

"Can I try that? I won't be that fast, but it's a cool move," Kiri said.

"Sure!" Finn gave her a wide grin. "I'm happy to let you steal my moves if it makes us better."

"Borrow. Not steal," Kiri said.

"We can all share," Grey said with a smile. "Thanks for leading practice today, Finn. You should do it more often. We could use some fresh ideas—some more offensive ones."

"Really?" Finn sounded like he didn't quite believe Grey, and it made Grey feel bad. Maybe he'd been suppressing Finn's talents.

Grey nodded. "If my ideas can't beat Lam, maybe yours will. Lam and I are too similar. You see the game differently."

"True, but if they get Hazel . . ." Finn usually tried to play it cool, but even he looked worried by the prospect. "They'll have a good offensive player then. And she'll teach them stuff like this, too, if they let her."

Kiri let out a long sigh. "I wish she would just stay."

"Me too," Grey said. But the longer it took Hazel to let them know, the more it felt like she wasn't coming back. He tried to tell himself that at least they knew what was going on this time, but it didn't help.

"Looks like we're about to find out one way or the other." Finn pointed to the south.

Hazel was walking toward them. She was still a little far off, but by the slow way she walked, Grey had a feeling he knew what she was going to say.

CHAPTER 8

Grey, Kiri, and Finn jumped down from the tower to meet Hazel and learn their fate. They met her on the riverbank, and she wouldn't look Grey in the eyes. He knew his worries were coming true. He took a deep breath and said, "You're going with Lam, right?"

Hazel nodded. "I'm sorry, but I need that spot home. I already told you why. If your ranks drop a bit and mine goes up because of Lam, then I have it. I can't pass up this chance even if I do feel bad about leaving you guys. I hate to say it, but you really grew on me, Pip-squeak."

By the way she said, "Pip-squeak," Grey knew it wasn't meant to be mean. Hazel said it the way a big sister would, and it almost made Grey tear up. He was mad that she wouldn't see it through with them, but he couldn't force anyone to stay in the squad. And he didn't want more drama than had already come their way. Grey needed to focus on what to do next, not how to change something he couldn't.

So he said, "Good luck, Hazel."

Hazel nodded. "You too, guys."

They watched Hazel walk away, and Grey felt like their chances at the top five were going with her. But he wasn't about to say that. He moved on to another topic. "Well, I guess we gotta talk about Ben and Tristan now."

Finn groaned. "Can we not? I'm done with drama tonight."

"Maybe tomorrow?" Kiri offered. "We can't hold off long on discussing it, unfortunately. There's only a week and a half left until the end of the season."

"First thing tomorrow morning," Grey said. "We can all think about what we can do and offer suggestions. I don't really know what is best at this point."

Finn and Kiri agreed, and they headed back to the cabins since it was nearly time for their mandatory rest period. When Grey stepped inside his cabin, Ben and Tristan were already in there. They were clearly waiting for him.

Ben stood up from where he sat on his bed. "Word has it that Hazel went with Lam."

Grey nodded.

"Have you . . . decided if you want to ally with us?" Ben asked.

Grey shook his head. "We're sleeping on it. We'll find you tomorrow before battles."

"Okay, cool," Ben said.

Grey laid down on his bed and closed his eyes, though he wouldn't fall asleep until the game made him. But it would send a message that he didn't want to talk. He needed to think about whether or not an alliance with Ben and Tristan would help. If they couldn't be in the same squad, what could they really do to help each other?

The next day, Grey's squad met in the forest. Grey leaned on the barrier, folding his arms as he said, "I know Finn won't like it, but I'm not opposed to being allies with Ben and Tristan. They left us, and they did it in a mean way, but I know how badly they want to get home. If I had to pick any veterans to go home this season, it would be them."

"I agree," Kiri said. "I wish they hadn't betrayed us, but I'm not gutted over it anymore."

Finn sighed. "I guess I'm cool with it as long as they don't get in our way. Honestly, it doesn't seem like they're that good."

"They take directions well," Grey said. "And they practice hard. So I was thinking that as part of being allies, they could practice with us."

Kiri nodded. "We can't talk to them in battles, so what else can we do?"

"If we know what skins they're wearing, we can avoid them," Finn suggested. "Or they can start on one side of the map and us on the other."

Grey thought about that for a moment. "Do you think that would be considered cheating?"

Finn shrugged.

"Maybe Ben and Tristan would know," Kiri offered.

"Or they would tell us what benefitted them," Finn said.

"I think knowing their skins might be pushing it," Grey said. "But if we agreed to land with one of our teams at the start of the bus's path and the other at the end . . . then we'd at least avoid each other for a little bit of time. That wouldn't be so bad, would it? It's not like we'd be teaming up on others. And we wouldn't be able to fully avoid eliminating each other. It would be delayed is all."

Finn pursed his lips as he thought about it. "As long as we get to leave the bus first, I'm okay with that."

Grey nodded. "Let's see what they think. I told them to wait in the battle warehouse."

Grey's squad headed over to meet Ben and Tristan. The two boys waited at a table, looking like they were about to take a hard test at school. Their demeanors didn't improve when they spotted Grey.

"So?" Ben asked when Grey, Finn, and Kiri sat at the table with them. "What's the verdict?"

"We were thinking of letting you come to our practices," Grey started. "And then in game . . . it's tricky, but what if we agree to start at opposite ends of whatever path the bus takes each battle? We'd take the early launch, and you the later one. We could avoid each other for a while at least, but any more than that and I worry we'd be accused of cheating."

Tristan nodded. "You did report Zach—anyone would be waiting for you to slip up so they could report you back."

"I'm not interested in cheating anyway," Grey said. "But I do want to help you guys get home if I can."

"Thanks, man," Ben said with a small smile. "I think that's a pretty fair alliance . . . though maybe it favors us more than you."

Grey shrugged. "Maybe, but knowing one good duo isn't close doesn't hurt. And we need practice partners who aren't going to sabotage us."

"You better not." Finn leaned forward, glaring at both of them. "We're your only hope at getting a better rank after all this. There's only ten days left. You both know you're out of time to make more drama, right?"

"We know," Tristan said. "I'd offer to give you Zach's strategies to prove we're not going back, but I know you won't want them."

"You're right." Grey held his hand out to Ben. "So we got a deal?"

Ben glanced at Tristan for confirmation. Tristan gave a quick nod, and then Ben took Grey's hand. "It's a deal."

Grey put his hand in front of Tristan next. "You shake, too."

Tristan looked hesitant.

"You don't have to be like this," Grey said. "I'm not mad at you. I really do get it. Maybe it won't be the same as before, but we can still be friends, can't we?"

"Yeah." Tristan took Grey's hand and for the first time really looked him in the eye. "Thank you, Grey."

"Thank you for teaching me all the good loot routes," Grey replied. "I wouldn't have gotten this far without either of you, and I'm not about to forget that. I hope you're the last two we eliminate in every battle after this."

Tristan grinned. "We'll get you a couple times at least."

"We'll be lucky to even get top ten without Hazel," Finn grumbled.

"Since when were you the insecure one?" Kiri asked. "What happened to overly confident Finn?"

"This place," he replied.

"Yeah, it has that effect," Ben said.

Grey put his hand on Finn's shoulder, knowing that Finn must finally be getting homesick. It took Finn longer to realize this place was more like a prison than a game, but Grey would help him get out soon. "We can do this together. Even if we have to get through Hazel and the rest of Lam's squad to do it."

Finn stared at his hands, looking sad. "Maybe . . ."

Battles begin in thirty seconds!

Grey waited for the teleport, even if it would only move him a few yards to the ranked line. Teleporting had gotten so normal that he might miss it once he got back to the real world. It didn't make him feel sick like it first had, and it was super convenient.

"Welcome to Day Fifty-Two of Battles!" the Admin said when she appeared. "With ten days until the new season begins, we would like to encourage all of you to keep playing as best as you can. While many of you have determined correctly that going home will not be possible for you this season, playing your best in battles is another form of practice that will improve your play and prepare you for next season."

Grey heard several people in the line snicker at this suggestion. It wasn't as if the Admin could make them play well, but he did worry some would take her words to heart. While fighting the top players was difficult, it was nice to be able to pick off everyone else.

"Speaking of continuing to improve play," the Admin continued, "many of you are not utilizing the practice area anymore. Please consider how valuable practice is. Many of the top players this season are dedicated to practicing, and they didn't give up when things got difficult. This could be you next season."

"Oh, come on! You already trapped us here, and now you're telling us how to spend our free time?" someone yelled from the lower-ranked area of the line. "Quit lecturing us and get to the stupid battles."

The Admin sighed. "The advice was well-intentioned. Good luck in today's battles."

Grey closed his eyes, waiting for the familiar sound of the battle bus chugging along through the sky. He told himself today would go well. It had to. There was no more room for bad ranks.

CHAPTER 9

Despite the alliance, the day did not go well for Grey's squad. He'd hoped that, because Hazel did care about them, she would somehow convince Lam to go easy on Grey. That was not what happened.

"Do they all have tommy guns? This is ridiculous!" Finn yelled as he furiously put up walls to protect him from the unending bullet spam.

"I'm almost out of mats," Kiri said. "We're not healing our way out of this."

Grey could only sigh. He was out of materials as well. The last battle had gone on for ten minutes. They had landed in Snobby Shores this time and had run into Lam's squad in Pleasant Park as they tried to get to the next storm circle.

Grey's squad hadn't farmed up enough yet ... and somehow Lam's squad was looted up with every SMG in the game. The rapid fire was impossible to survive when there were four players using it.

"I'm almost out of mats, too," Finn said. "Get ready to shoot and pray."

"Focus, Hazel," Grey said as he pulled out his shotgun. Not because he was mad at her, but because she still wore her signature skin—the girl with the green pigtails. She'd be easy to see and aim for. He couldn't guess which avatar was Lam's, otherwise he'd pick her. "Maybe we can get her eliminated at least."

Once Finn's last wall fell, Grey aimed at Hazel. The shot hit, but it did hardly any damage. She must have been low after they all hit her, but Grey's squad fell before Hazel did. Then it was over. Grey cursed the shotgun nerf once again. Sometimes the weapon would come through and do the damage it used to, but never when he needed it most.

"Ugh, they put us in the top fifteen again!" Kiri said.

"Yeah . . ." At the beginning of the season, he would have thought ranking in the top fifteen for a battle was amazing, but at this point it felt like he may as well have died first. Being in the top fifteen wouldn't push up their average. It was one more battle with no progress, finishing a whole day of battles they didn't win.

It didn't matter if they had an alliance. They didn't have Hazel, and that was what would come back to bite them in the end. Grey had told himself he wasn't mad at her, but in that moment he was.

Lam's squad won the last Victory Royale of the day, and when they all appeared in the battle warehouse again, Lam's squad congratulated themselves on how they'd won every game of the day. Hazel had already jumped ahead of Grey in rank with those five victories. Grey didn't even hear what the Admin had to say, he was so mad about it, and when he could move he charged right for his favorite spot in the forest.

When he got there, he kicked at the barrier and yelled, "Can't I ever catch a break? Ugh!"

"Do you really want one?" Tae Min's voice came from behind.

Grey wasn't in the mood for Tae Min's cryptic conversations. He turned and glared at him. "Of course I want one. I'm so freaking tired of this."

"Are you?" Tae Min asked.

"Yes!" Grey yelled back. "Stop asking me dumb questions! You know everything anyway because you can read minds or something. What do *you* want, Tae Min? That's a question no one knows the answer to!"

Somewhere in the back of Grey's mind, he knew he shouldn't be yelling at Tae Min. He felt bad, but he probably would have yelled at who- ever came to see him. Tae Min just happened to be the one to show up.

"What I really want?" Tae Min said as he walked closer to Grey. "I want to know why, this entire time, you've never asked me to be on your squad. You're the only person who has never asked even after all our talks."

Grey glared at him. "How could I ask when you told me everyone just wants stuff from you? I didn't want to be the same. Besides, I figured if you ever wanted to be on anyone's squad you'd tell them you were joining. It's not like anyone here would say no."

Tae Min smiled. This time it was a real smile, big and wide enough to surprise Grey. Then Tae Min said, "Well then, I would like to join your squad."

Grey blinked a few times. He couldn't have heard right. "You would?"

"I'm still not going home," Tae Min said. "But yes, I want to help you get there, as long as you can accept that I will eliminate myself before we hit the top ten each match. I will have to coach you from spectator mode after that."

"Okay, you're in." Grey knew the rest of his squad wouldn't protest. Having Tae Min play with them? It didn't sound real. "What about practices?"

"I'll teach you what you need to know. All of you, even Ben and Tristan," Tae Min said. "Ideally, I'd like to get you, Kiri, Finn, Ben, and Tristan into the top five, but I'm afraid I can't guarantee that with two separate squads."

Grey felt a twist in his stomach. "Not Hazel?"

"If there were a top six, that would work, but there isn't," Tae Min said.

"Right." Grey stared at his shoes, which still looked the same as the day he came, even though he'd traipsed through the virtual woods for nearly two months. "It's just . . . Hazel doesn't have anyone on the outside. She's really scared she'll end up like Robert."

Grey had tried his best not to think about

how Robert had died in real life. The Admin claimed it was of natural causes, but still. One day he was here playing, and the next he was gone. It was too scary. Grey didn't want that to happen to anyone else.

"I see . . ." Tae Min rubbed his chin as he thought. "Well, if one of you wants to give up your spot, we can work that out."

Grey gulped. How could Grey ask anyone to do that? Could he do it? He should do it . . . "Let's think about that later. Are you sure we can still rank in the top five? It seems harder and harder to move up in rank with all the battles averaging out."

"I don't have complete control," Tae Min said. "But I believe it's possible if your squad or Ben and Tristan take all the victories from here on out."

"All?" Grey would have loved to win every game, but it didn't seem possible even with Tae Min's help.

Tae Min nodded. "Tomorrow will be the most difficult, since I only have tonight to help you practice. But after that, it should improve rapidly."

Grey had to believe him, because so far

everything Tae Min said had been right. And if he hadn't been tanking his rank on purpose, he'd still be ranked first instead of in the top twenty. If anyone could help them win the rest of the games, it was Tae Min. "Okay, then let's get to work."

"Meet at the ghost town with everyone. I'll be in the saloon. We'll take care of squading then as well." Tae Min walked away.

Grey waited for several minutes before he moved. For some reason, it felt like he still needed to keep his friendship with Tae Min secret. If people found out right now that Tae Min planned to join Grey's squad, they would lose it. Their enemies would figure it out eventually, but they would underestimate Grey in the meantime. And being underestimated was the best place to be. Surprising an overly confident opponent almost always resulted in success.

After his wait, Grey headed out to find his friends. It was hard not to run and give away his excitement.

Grey spotted Kiri, Finn, Ben, and Tristan outside of the practice warehouse. Even though Grey had stomped off, they had grouped together to practice. From the looks of it, they were trying to survive SMG spam and find an opening to counterattack.

"Are you done sulking already?" Kiri asked.

"We thought you'd be gone all evening," Finn said. "Sorry for practicing without you."

"Don't worry about it," Grey said as a big smile spread across his face.

They all gave him a strange look, but it was Ben who said, "What's with the smile?"

"He's lost it, mates," Kiri said. "I worried this would happen."

Grey shook his head. "No, I haven't. Grab your best weapons and follow me."

"Okay . . ." Tristan looked skeptical. They all did, but they still did as Grey asked. Then they headed out past the fields and forests to the ghost town. It looked just as abandoned as ever. Lam never practiced here, since she preferred to build her own structures rather than use what was around her. He'd seen the others in the top fifteen closer to the practice warehouse.

Grey went right for the saloon. It was the first place he'd practiced with Ben and Tristan, and it felt right to be back here with them for the most important practice of their lives.

"I don't know if hide-and-seek will help us at this point," Tristan said.

"Well, it might with the right coach." Grey opened the saloon doors and stepped inside.

Tae Min sat on the bar, his feet planted on a chair. He gave them a clever grin. "Hey, everyone."

"Meet our new squad member," Grey said. "He's gonna teach us how to win every game."

Grey's friends stood there shocked for at least ten seconds. Grey held in his laugh, though it was funny to see their wide eyes and dropped jaws.

Finally, Kiri was able to utter, "No. Way."

"It's true." Tae Min hopped off the bar, and an AR appeared in his hands like magic, though Grey knew he'd just equipped it from his inventory. "Looks like Grey doesn't go around bragging about our friendship even to his closest allies. That's what I like about him."

"F-Friends?" Ben managed to say. He looked at Grey. "Is that why you're so good? How long have you been holding out on us?"

"He wasn't holding out," Tae Min said for Grey. "He is good because he is talented. I am his friend because he never saw me as a golden ticket to freedom. Funny how that makes me want to help, but it does."

"Wow." Finn punched Grey's shoulder. "I don't care how this happened. I'm so pumped to level up!"

"Good," Tae Min said. "Let's get started. We don't have time to waste."

CHAPTER 10

Grey and his friends were more than ready to learn from Tae Min. It seemed unreal, watching him pace in front of them. He sized them up one by one. Grey wondered if they looked as young and ragtag as he felt in that moment. Tae Min was older, cooler, and more skilled than them by miles.

Tae Min's black hair partially hid his eyes, and he pushed it back before he said, "Today's lesson: anticipating enemy movement. Most players focus their energy on what they would do, but it's essential that you learn how the opponent moves. And more importantly, you must learn how to manipulate them into doing what you want. This will put them right where you want, and then . . ."

Tae Min equipped his sniper and aimed right at Grey. He didn't shoot, but he didn't have to for Grey to feel like he'd have been eliminated immediately.

"So you do read minds," Finn said.

"Not exactly," Tae Min replied. "But you can call it that if you'd like. Will you play victim, Finn, since you seem so eager?"

"Victim?" Finn shot a glare at Tae Min. "That confidence."

"Finn," Kiri said. "Stop acting like you can beat him and learn something."

"Fine," Finn grumbled. "I'll play 'victim.'"

"Good." Tae Min stepped back, and Finn followed him to the open area of the saloon. Grey and the rest of his friends stayed near the door to watch. "Now, standing here, what is the easiest way to eliminate me?"

Finn gave him a confused look. "Is this a trick question?"

Tae Min shook his head.

"Shoot." Finn said as he held up his weapon.

"Right. Go for it," Tae Min instructed.

Finn didn't hesitate, and he even aimed up in

anticipation of Tae Min jumping to avoid the shot. But Tae Min did something Grey hadn't seen anyone do. Tae Min crouched. Finn's shot flew over Tae Min's head and damaged the wall behind him. Meanwhile, Tae Min shot Finn in return.

"What the—?" Finn said.

"This game is a lot like the video game of Fortnite," Tae Min said. "But it's not *exactly* the same, is it?"

"No," Grey said as it clicked. "You have to press a button to crouch or jump in the game . . . here, we don't have buttons."

"Exactly," Tae Min said as he stood. "In the normal game, most people spend all their time jumping because it's an easier button to press. They don't crouch because the button is less convenient. Here, the movements take the same amount of effort, but people still favor jumping. Finn even aimed to compensate for the assumption that I would jump."

"I never thought of that," Ben said. "It's such a small thing, but it could save you if you know your enemy is aiming high."

"Yes," Tae Min said. "Now, the next basic principle. Finn, you played a great victim. Kiri, would you like to join me for this one?"

Kiri gulped. "S-Sure."

Finn stepped back next to Grey. "Crouching… I feel like an idiot."

"Don't," Grey said. "We're all here to learn. I didn't think of that either."

Tae Min placed a wooden wall between him and Kiri. "Now, Kiri, what is the easiest way to eliminate me with this wall in the way?"

"Uhh . . ." Kiri stood there for too long, unsure of the easiest way.

Grey wanted to jump in because he knew what he would do. He'd build his own ramp onto the wall and attack from above. He was sure that was what Tae Min would say, too, because going around the side would take longer. But he knew it was important for everyone here to learn.

Kiri backed up instead of building, and then she threw a C4 and exploded it. It destroyed everything around Tae Min, him included, and left a big hole in the ceiling of the saloon.

That was not what Grey expected.

Tae Min began to laugh. "Okay, okay, you got me. That *is* faster than what I had in mind. Smart move, though delayed."

"Thanks." Kiri beamed. "I know we won't always have C4. What were you going to do?"

Tae Min looked at Grey. "Your turn. I think you know what I am looking for."

Grey and Kiri switched spots. Tae Min put up another wall, and Grey didn't hesitate to build the ramp and start moving up. But before he could take a shot, Tae Min placed a wall right in Grey's face. The surprise flustered Grey, and he moved to his right in hopes to get a shot from that side.

Another wall went up.

Grey moved to the left, but Tae Min wasn't there. The next thing Grey knew, he took a shot to the back. Tae Min had run around the right wall to attack. And it was only after the quick movement that Grey understood what had happened.

"You put me where you wanted," Grey said. "How . . . ?"

"Most good players know the fastest, most efficient ways to eliminate players," Tae Min said as he looked behind Grey. "How many of you would have built that ramp up?"

Ben and Tristan raised their hands, clearly gobsmacked by watching Tae Min work. Finn reluctantly added his own hand.

"You were surprised, right, Grey?" Tae Min asked.

Grey nodded.

"When people are caught off guard, they tend to act out of instinct," Tae Min continued. "Since you are right-handed, I can assume you would move right without thinking of which direction would be better . . . They seem equally good in the moment. Once I blocked the right side, you'll consider the left side the best choice. So you moved that way, but knowing that I came from the right. This will give me the best shot, even if you had the instinct to turn around, I would still have the advantage."

"What if Grey had built up?" Tristan asked. "If he'd gained high ground, he might have a better spot."

"I considered that," Tae Min said. "If he had, I would have moved up the stairs to catch him on the second floor."

"Riiiiight," Ben said. "Smart."

"It would be different if we were out in the open," Tae Min said. "You are not completely wrong—it's very situational. Today we're focusing on tight quarters. I need to prepare you for Tilted Towers."

Grey's eyes went wide. "Oh, I didn't realize you'd want us to land there."

"It has the best loot," Finn said. "And a lot of it. That's why I keep telling you to go there. If you survive, you have all the best stuff to fight with."

"Yeah, but it's so unpredictable," Grey insisted.

"It's incredibly predictable if you know how other players will behave," Tae Min replied. "Which is why I'm teaching you. Don't worry, we won't land there until I know you're ready. And right now, you're not."

"Okay." Though Grey was afraid of Tilted Towers, he did trust that Tae Min would teach them to play better. And if Tae Min thought they were ever ready to take on Tilted Towers, Grey would have to believe him.

CHAPTER 11

Grey and his friends practiced their hearts out under the guidance of Tae Min. It was a different style of teaching compared to Grey's style—which was a lot of real-world simulation practice. Tae Min instead focused on step-by-step instruction and discussion. He was constantly asking them to think about what they would do and didn't demand as much actual doing.

But Grey believed it would help them because he was already seeing the game differently. He was imagining how he would face various players and what he could do to push them into the plays he wanted them to make. He was concocting his own ways to counterattack after he'd gotten the enemy right where he wanted.

If they could execute this in battle, they would definitely win more.

He was glad Tae Min would be in their squad to advise them, because Grey already knew he wouldn't be able to adapt these concepts overnight.

Five minutes until mandatory rest!

"All right, Grey, squad me," Tae Min said. "We'll pick up practice in between every battle tomorrow."

"Sounds good," Grey said as he extended the invitation. When Tae Min accepted it, Grey could hardly believe that the top player's name was listed with the rest of his squad. He didn't feel like he deserved it, but he wasn't about to turn Tae Min away at this point. Not only was Tae Min brilliant, but Grey liked hanging out with him. Tae Min was much nicer than anyone would assume from his quiet and aloof appearance.

They headed back to the practice warehouse, and Grey grew more nervous as Tae Min stayed with them. People would definitely notice, since Tae Min never hung out with anyone.

"You're nervous," Tae Min said. "Do you want me to hide?"

"I wasn't sure you'd want to be seen with us. Also, I wondered if the element of surprise might help us tomorrow," Grey admitted.

"Besides, walking with us would definitely ruin your reputation," Finn added.

Tae Min smirked. "I appreciate that you're thinking strategy, but in this case I believe I'm better used as an intimidation factor and not a surprise. If you haven't noticed, everyone is afraid of me."

"True," Kiri said. "When you were still playing at the top, even the thought that you might be around changed the way we played. It's probably the same for everyone else."

Tae Min nodded. "They will try to implement new strategies to counter me. Untested strategies also mean they won't be playing comfortably. They will play worse."

"I see," Grey said. His squad was used to being underestimated, so he'd never thought of the power of letting players know Tae Min was with them. It was a completely different mindset, and Grey was glad Tae Min was familiar with it.

Grey spotted Zach and Hui Yin as they entered the practice warehouse from the north doors. They were discussing something near the weapon racks.

Sure enough, the moment Zach saw them, his eyes filled with terror. Hui Yin turned to see what had scared Zach so much, and soon she looked just as scared.

Tae Min just kept walking, so Grey's squad did the same. Quiet settled over the open field in front of the warehouse as they made their way out there. Vlad and Yuri glared at them, while Lam's group looked horrified. Grey tried not to look at Hazel, who would definitely be upset by Grey's replacement squad member. None of them could have guessed that this would happen. Not even Grey had, though now that he thought about it, Tae Min had given him plenty of chances to ask for help.

The shocked stares didn't stop in the practice area. Even those who'd given up for the season couldn't help but watch Grey and his friends. But these people weren't silent; they whispered among themselves about what it could mean. About whether or not Tae Min was finally going to leave the game. He'd never helped so many people at once.

They wouldn't get an answer. Grey hated

people gossiping about him, but Tae Min ignored all of it and didn't care.

Their group stopped in front of Grey's cabin, and Tae Min said, "Meet up in the same place first thing tomorrow morning."

"Sweet as, mates," Kiri said and then headed for her cabin with a big smile on her face.

"I wish we could switch cabins," Finn said as he took a few steps back. "I'm the odd one out now. My roomies are boring."

"Sorry," Grey said. "I wish we could switch, too."

Finn waved as he left, and the rest of them went into their cabin. Lorenzo wasn't there yet, but he would be soon. Grey wondered if it would be weird. He and Lorenzo had become friendly, but he wouldn't say they were that close, either.

"I just have one question," Tristan said as they all went to their beds. "If Tae Min is in Grey's squad, then how will we get help? We won't be able to hear his directions."

"Don't worry," Tae Min said. "I will teach you how to get to the end. It'll be boring, but it'll work."

Tristan did not seem comforted by this.

"Maybe once we get the hang of things, Tae

Min can switch back and forth between our squads?" Grey suggested.

Tae Min raised an eyebrow. "You're okay with that?"

Grey nodded. "We all need to get home. After a few days, I might be able to get a feel for what you'd do based on the battles we've already done. Then you could switch to Ben and Tristan's until they get a good feel and switch back to us."

"That might work. I should've expected this from you," Tac Min said. "Still so generous even after everything."

Grey wasn't sure that was a compliment or not, but he decided to take it as one.

"Thanks, Grey," Ben said. "You don't have to offer that after everything we've done, but you are just that awesome."

"Stop, guys." Grey put his pillow over his head, feeling self-conscious over the praise. "Just do your best and don't waste this chance."

"We won't," Tristan said. "We've fought too long for this."

Thirty seconds until mandatory rest!

Lorenzo burst into the room and dove for his bed. Before the last seconds ticked down, he said, "You guys all suck, by the way, leaving me out."

Grey felt bad, but there was nothing to say before his vision went to black and he was forced to rest like everyone else. Tomorrow would be a new day, a day full of victories if all went well.

CHAPTER 12

Just before it was time for battles, Tae Min gathered Grey and his friends into a circle. "Good practice, everyone. Remember what I've taught you, because as you know I will get eliminated before the end of the game. You can still do it. Don't be intimidated by anyone."

"Easy for you to say," Ben said. "What if I can't even hide right? Me and Tristan can't afford any losses under the top ten."

"You'll be fine," Tae Min said. "Give yourself some credit, Ben. Your weakness isn't skill—it's self-doubt."

Ben took a deep breath. "Okay. Thanks."

"Grey's squad will land at Retail Row," Tae Min said. "Ben's squad will land at Haunted

Hills where there won't be much action. Move for the circle and stay in safe positions."

"Got it," Grey said loudly. They had already worked out that people would be spying on them this morning, so they were giving out fake landing places. Grey's squad would really be landing at Salty Springs while Ben and Tristan were directed to land at Lonely Lodge.

Thirty seconds until battles begin!

Today it felt like forever waiting for the teleport to take them to the battle warehouse. Grey was eager to play, which he hadn't felt in a long time. Not just because they had Tae Min, but because Grey wanted to try the things he'd learned. He hoped it would make a big difference.

Grey's vision went black and he appeared in the battle warehouse. He looked at the rankings on the wall and told himself they would go up today. Because they would get five Victory Royales like Tae Min said they would. Grey had gotten three in one day before—surely a full sweep was possible now.

"Welcome to Day Fifty-Three of Battles!" the Admin said. "Just for your information, the developers have reviewed the impact of some recent alterations to various weapons. They are currently working on finding a happy medium to improve play. Please be patient as we determine what is best for you and for the game. Good luck in today's battles!"

"Does that mean buffs to the ARs and shotguns?" Kiri asked as they all appeared in the Battle Bus.

"Probably," Finn said. "Since they've both been nerfed way too much. It's all SMG spam now, and that dang tommy gun . . ."

"It made being solo much more difficult," Tae Min said. "A squad with SMGs is obscene."

"What they should do is nerf explosives," Kiri said.

"I agree," Grey said. "Too much damage and too much max ammo."

It was nice to talk like this because it took Grey's mind off the serious task ahead of them. Since Tae Min was in charge this time, Grey didn't know what to do with himself. He'd gotten so used to being the leader, he wondered if he'd forgotten how to follow. Finn and Hazel had made plenty of mistakes because they were used to doing their own thing instead of listening—Grey didn't want to fall into that.

"Here we go," Tae Min said as he jumped from the bus.

Grey scrambled to follow him, not realizing he'd just jumped without a countdown or anything. Kiri and Finn jumped after he did. There wasn't too much of a gap between all of them, but Grey worried the delay could mean an enemy got a weapon before they did.

"You gotta count it off, man!" Finn said over the coms. "You're not solo anymore!"

"It's better to land scattered," Tae Min said. "Then people can't tell if you're a squad or not."

"Oh . . ." Grey had never thought of that, either. They had changed their avatar's skins often to prevent being identified, but if they were grouped in the landing position, then people could tell they were together. Now, onlookers might not assume all four of them were grouped up. They could be duos or solos for all anyone knew. "Wish I'd figured that out sooner."

"Spread out and loot. Call if you need help," Tae Min said, and they dove for Salty Springs. "I'm taking the blue house."

"I'll grab brick," Finn replied.

"Small house for me," Kiri said.

"Then I'll go for the broken house." Grey aimed his glider for the house he'd picked. As he broke open the roof, he scanned the area for other players. There were at least four, but they were grouped in twos, so they were likely duos. They hadn't landed in the same place as Grey, but his squad would have to take them down before leaving Salty Springs.

Grey opened the first chest he came across, only to find a disappointing basic pistol plus bandages and ammo. What he needed was a shield to increase his armor. There wasn't much to be done with bandages unless he lost health.

He broke down furniture and the floor to get down from the attic into the second level of the house. Another chest sat on a desk in a room. Grey didn't get much better stuff from that one—just a blue shotgun, ammo, and some hand grenades. If those enemies decided to push him, he might be in some trouble.

"A legendary scar, sweet!" Finn said. "Anyone need shields? I found a bunch in this house."

"Full shield here," Kiri reported.

"Me," Grey said with relief. "Only bandages and sad weapons in my place."

"That's the way of the road, isn't it?" Finn said. "Either lucky or not."

"You can always make do," Tae Min said.

"I'm pushing the duo in my house. Kiri, back me up while Finn and Grey even out their loot."

Grey finished up looting his house while Finn came to him. He was happy to at least get his hands on a green AR and an LMG out of the last chests. While Finn handed over the shields, the notifications read:

Tae Min knocked down Anya.

Kiri eliminated Veejay.

Tae Min eliminated Anya.

"Nice job," Tae Min said. "Next pair."

"Shouldn't we wait for Grey and Finn?" Kiri asked.

"No, they need to farm materials while we do this so we don't lose time," Tae Min said.

Grey took that as a cue to start farming, and Finn joined in breaking down whatever they could inside their current house. Then they ran outside and farmed the trees, fences, and rocks for more building fodder.

Tae Min eliminated Petra.

Kiri eliminated Eric by head shot.

"Nice one, Kiri," Tae Min said. "I need to get you home before you steal my title of best sniper."

Kiri laughed. "Your true motivation surfaces."

Grey hated breaking down the cars because they sounded loud alarms, but he wondered if Tae Min might want them to have metal. "The cars, too?"

"Yeah," Tae Min said. "Maybe the sound will lure players here. Then we can take their loot."

Grey did as he was told, though he never thought it was a good idea to lure players to him. He was usually trying to avoid enemies. Grey supposed Tae Min enjoyed fighting, especially when he usually always won and didn't mind facing a lot of players in quick succession.

Sure enough, a few people showed up from the direction of the Fatal Fields after all the racket Grey's squad made. The enemies were quickly eliminated, providing a lot of items to choose from.

"Who needs to loot when others can do it for you?" Finn said with a laugh.

"Exactly," Tae Min said.

The early game went too smoothly, and Grey knew it was because of Tae Min. It was strange to follow him around and witness the way he moved through the fights. Every encounter felt like second nature to Tae Min. He would guide them through it easily, and sometimes he could even tell who they were fighting just based on how the enemy players moved.

Before Grey knew it, they had cycled through Retail Row and Tomato Town, eliminating people left and right.

But Grey knew this wouldn't last forever. The number of people in the battle dwindled, and that meant it would soon be time for Tae Min to eliminate himself. He would still be giving them directions from spectator mode, but suddenly Grey worried it might not be enough.

"All right, top fifteen now," Tae Min. "You ready for end game, Grey?"

"Honestly? No," Grey said. "I can't do what you just did. That was flawless."

"You can do it," Tae Min said. "You have done it many times already. I'll get you through the sticky parts."

"We got this, Grey," Finn said.

"We have plenty of gear," Kiri said. "Ben and Tristan are still out there, too. Everything is going well. Have some confidence."

"Okay, okay," Grey said as he tried to muster all the confidence he could. "I'm ready when you are, Tae Min."

"Wait here," Tae Min said. He began to build

a ramp up into the sky, and then he jumped off the top.

Tae Min had a great fall.

"Grab the loot," Grey said as they gathered around Tae Min's items. With the extra materials, Grey was maxed out in wood, brick, and metal now.

"The circle will eventually close over Dusty Divot," Tae Min said. "Head there now."

"Got it." Grey was determined to win the Victory Royale they desperately needed.

CHAPTER 13

Before Grey's remaining squad members even got close to Dusty Divot, Grey could see the tower jutting out of the crater. He stopped running and took cover in a small shed. "You saw that, right, Tae Min?"

"Yeah," he replied. "Looks like Lam beat us there."

"She *always* beats us there if she makes it to late game," Kiri said.

"She'll see us coming from a mile away," Finn grumbled.

Grey tried to think positively, but they'd faced this situation before at Dusty Divot, and Lam had always gotten the best of them. He didn't know what play would work. "What should we do, Tae Min?"

"Lam likes to build towers and look down on people," Tae Min said. "She might not be looking up."

Grey immediately caught on. "Are you saying we should sky base this?"

"You have launch pads," Tae Min replied. "Come at them from above and they won't see it, especially if people are approaching from below."

There were still twelve left in the game, so there was a chance that others would be headed for Dusty Divot from a different direction. They could be a distraction. But it was still risky, since building that high meant one rogue rocket could take down their whole structure.

"Let's do it," Finn said. "We have plenty of materials. We don't have to build too close to Lam's tower—we just need to get up high enough to be able to glide down on them."

"Okay," Grey said as he peeked out the shed's window. He took in their surroundings, trying to decide the best place for this sky base. His eyes settled on the perfect spot—a big mountain north of Tomato Town. It would be in the storm soon, which would mean less chance of someone breaking the base.

"That's the place," Tae Min said. "Better get running."

"Where?" Kiri asked.

"Follow me," Grey said. Tae Min was obviously spectating from Grey's point of view right now, since he could see the mountain Grey settled on. They left the shed and ran. Since they had eliminated so many players in that area already, Grey wasn't too worried about someone sniping them.

"Storm's coming in thirty seconds," Kiri said.

"We might be in it for a little bit, but we can handle it." Grey began to build ramps to get up the mountain faster. He hoped Lam wouldn't be able to see their building from this far away. As Grey looked toward Dusty Divot, he couldn't see her tower from this distance. That was a good sign.

Once they got to the top of the mountain, Tae Min said, "Finn, take over building. Do a one-by-one for seven stories and then ramp up toward Dusty until I tell you to stop."

"On it." Finn began to build while Grey and Kiri kept close to him so they could jump up to the next ramp he would build in the tower. The storm hit them, and their health began to tick down. After they were seven stories up like Tae Min directed, Finn started on the ramps. He built them three wide so there was less chance of them being shot out of the sky.

Soon they were back inside the safe zone, but they had all taken half their health in damage. They paused to use their one campfire to recover health before trudging forward.

"How much higher?" Finn asked as he switched from brick to metal materials. "I don't have much left."

"Almost there," Tae Min said.

They were so high up, Grey could see nearly the entire island from where they were. Lam's tower didn't look so tall from this position, but he worried that Lam would see the sky base. They would hit maximum build height soon— anyone who looked up would spot them.

"Launch pad now," Tae Min said.

Finn built a flat floor for them, and Grey set down the launch pad. They jumped on it and shot into the air.

"Spread out," Tae Min directed. "Approach from different directions. If you see anyone, attack from behind."

Grey deployed his glider and moved away

from Kiri and Finn. The closer they got to the tower, the louder the gunfire sounded. There was definitely a battle going on down there because more walls and ramps appeared around the tower. Grey spotted a couple players who still looked like ants. They didn't fire at him or his squad because they were so focused on each other.

Hazel eliminated Zach.

Hazel eliminated Hui Yin.

Lam knocked down Vlad.

Trevor knocked down Ben.

"It's a mess down there!" Kiri said. "We gotta hurry before they get Ben eliminated."

"I got eyes on Hazel," Finn said. "She's trying to break a box."

"There's one over here on a box too," Grey said as he dove down closer. "I can't tell which box Ben and Tristan are in!"

"Doesn't matter! Get the attackers so Tristan can revive Ben," Tae Min said with a hint of stress in his voice for the first time. "Finn on Hazel. Grey, get the other attacker. Kiri, back them up from a sniper perch."

"Right," Kiri said as she landed on the top of the tower.

Grey swooped down on the player wearing

the zombie-girl skin, and the moment his feet touched the wooden floor, he equipped his SMG and opened fire. The player took all their shield damage before they turned around to attack. Grey crouched as Tae Min had taught them to, and the shotgun fire missed.

You knocked down Trevor.

With that notification, Grey knew Ben and Tristan were in the box near him, since that was who knocked down Ben. "Ben and Tristan are by me!"

Finn knocked down Hazel.

"Focus on Finn's side, Kiri!" Tae Min yelled. "Grey, find the rest of Lam's squad!"

Grey searched the mess of walls and ramps and floors, trying to see where the other two players were. He spotted movement a few stories above him and opened fire with his SMG. He had to break through the floor first, and the player fell to the next level.

"Push, Grey!" Tae Min commanded. "Finn, get in that box and take them out. Kiri, back Grey now."

"There's a player right below you, Kiri," Grey said as he built up to reach the enemy. "They're low."

"One behind you," Kiri said. "I got his shield off. He's hiding."

Finn eliminated Yuri.

Lam eliminated Vlad.

"Another duo down," Finn reported. "Moving to Grey's position."

"I got this one," Grey said as he reloaded his SMG. The player he was after had boxed herself in, and the SMG would burn down the walls she would build to defend herself. She only built three walls before she stopped—Grey realized she must have been out of materials. She started jumping around with her shotgun, landing a weak shot on Grey. He replied with his own shotgun.

You knocked down Lam.

Not three seconds after that, Finn was able to finish off Pilar, and the entire squad was eliminated. They were down to the final five, but it was a Victory Royale already because the only other two left were Ben and Tristan.

"I feel bad eliminating them," Grey said as he looked over to the box where they hid.

"Me too," Kiri admitted.

"I'll do it!" Finn ran over to the box, but just as he got there, Grey heard the clicking sound of two C4 being placed. Grey realized Ben and Tristan were about to take themselves out instead.

Kaboom!

Ben eliminated himself.

Tristan eliminated himself.

The explosion was just shy of hitting Finn when the Victory Royale was made official. It was only the first game of the day, but it felt good to start out on the right foot.

"On to the next one," Tae Min said when they all appeared back in the battle warehouse. "But first, more practice."

"Good thing you guys got there when you did," Ben said as they gathered together. "We were almost done for."

"Sorry about that," Grey said.

"No worries, it was still the best we did since Zach dropped us," Tristan said. "Thanks for helping even if we can't be in the same squad."

Grey smiled. Maybe this wasn't the exact way he pictured getting to the top five ranks, but at least he was still fighting for it with his friends. He had a feeling it would work out if they stuck together from now on.